INDIAN BOY

NK LIFE

good books are not to use ful/...................

Contents

Foreword

happy mind leat to meat

Acknowledgements

life is too shot

Prologue

Happy Boy is this book

India

India, officially the Republic of India (Hindi: Bhārat Gaṇarājya),[26] is a country in South Asia. It is the seventh-largest country by area, the second-most populous country, and the most populous democracy in the world. Bounded by the Indian Ocean on the south, the Arabian Sea on the southwest, and the Bay of Bengal on the southeast, it shares land borders with Pakistan to the west;[f] China, Nepal, and Bhutan to the north; and Bangladesh and Myanmar to the east. In the Indian Ocean, India is in the vicinity of Sri Lanka and the Maldives; its Andaman and Nicobar Islands share a maritime border with Thailand, Myanmar and Indonesia.

Modern humans arrived on the Indian subcontinent from Africa no later than 55,000 years ago.[27][28][29] Their long occupation, initially in varying forms of isolation as hunter-gatherers, has made the region highly diverse, second only to Africa in human genetic diversity.[30] Settled life emerged on the subcontinent in the western margins of the Indus river basin 9,000 years ago, evolving gradually into the Indus Valley Civilisation of the third millennium BCE.[31] By 1200 BCE, an archaic form of Sanskrit, an Indo-European language, had diffused into India from the northwest,[32][33] unfolding as the language of the Rigveda, and recording the dawning of Hinduism in India.[34] The Dravidian languages of India were supplanted in the northern and western regions.[35] By 400 BCE, stratification and exclusion by caste had emerged within Hinduism,[36] and Buddhism and Jainism had arisen, proclaiming social orders unlinked to heredity.[37] Early political consolidations gave rise to the loose-knit Maurya and Gupta Empires based in the Ganges Basin.[38] Their collective era was suffused with wide-ranging creativity,[39] but also marked by the declining status of women,[40] and the incorporation of untouchability into an organised system of belief.[g][41] In South India, the Middle kingdoms exported Dravidian-languages scripts and religious cultures to the kingdoms of Southeast Asia.[42]

In the early medieval era, Christianity, Islam, Judaism, and Zoroastrianism became established on India's southern and western coasts.[43] Muslim armies from Central Asia intermittently overran India's northern plains,[44] eventually founding the Delhi Sultanate, and drawing northern India into the cosmopolitan networks of medieval Islam.[45] In the 15th century, the Vijayanagara Empire created a long-lasting composite Hindu culture in south India.[46] In the Punjab, Sikhism emerged, rejecting institutionalised religion.[47] The Mughal Empire, in 1526, ushered in two centuries of relative peace,[48] leaving a legacy of luminous architecture.[h][49] Gradually expanding rule of the British East India Company followed, turning India into a colonial economy, but also consolidating its sovereignty.[50] British Crown rule began in 1858. The rights promised to Indians were granted slowly,[51][52] but technological changes were introduced, and ideas of education, modernity and the public life took root.[53] A pioneering and influential nationalist movement emerged, which was noted for nonviolent resistance and became the major factor in ending British rule.[54][55] In 1947 the British Indian Empire was partitioned into two independent dominions,[56][57][58][59] a Hindu-majority Dominion of India and a Muslim-majority Dominion of Pakistan, amid large-scale loss of life and an unprecedented migration.[60]

India has been a federal republic since 1950, governed in a democratic parliamentary system. It is a pluralistic, multilingual and multi-ethnic society. India's population grew from 361 million in 1951 to 1.211 billion in 2011.[61] During the same time, its nominal per capita income increased from US$64 annually to US$1,498, and its literacy rate from 16.6% to 74%. From being a comparatively destitute country in 1951,[62] India has become a fast-growing major economy and a hub for information technology services, with an expanding middle class.[63] It has a space programme which includes several planned or completed extraterrestrial missions. Indian movies, music, and spiritual teachings play an increasing role in global culture.[64] India has substantially reduced its rate of poverty, though at the cost of increasing economic inequality.[65] India is a nuclear-weapon state, which ranks high in military expenditure. It has disputes over Kashmir with its neighbours, Pakistan and China, unresolved since the mid-20th century.[66] Among the socio-economic challenges India faces are gender inequality, child malnutrition,[67] and rising levels of air pollution.[68] India's land is megadiverse, with four biodiversity hotspots.[69] Its forest cover comprises 21.7% of its area.[70] India's wildlife, which has traditionally been viewed with tolerance in India's culture,[71] is supported among these forests, and elsewhere, in protected habitats.

Contents

Etymology

Main article: Names of India

According to the Oxford English Dictionary (third edition 2009), the name "India" is derived from the Classical Latin India, a reference to South Asia and an uncertain region to its east; and in turn derived successively from: Hellenistic Greek India (Ἰνδία); ancient Greek Indos (Ἰνδός); Old Persian Hindush, an eastern province of the Achaemenid empire; and ultimately its cognate, the Sanskrit Sindhu, or "river," specifically the Indus River and, by implication, its well-settled southern basin.[72][73] The ancient Greeks referred to the Indians as Indoi (Ἰνδοί), which translates as "The people of the Indus".[74]

The term Bharat (Bhārat; pronounced [ˈbʱaːrət] (listen)), mentioned in both Indian epic poetry and the Constitution of India,[75][76] is used in its variations by many Indian languages. A modern rendering of the historical name Bharatavarsha, which applied originally to North India,[77][78] Bharat gained increased currency from the mid-19th century as a native name for India.[75][79]

Hindustan ([ɦɪndʊˈstaːn] (listen)) is a Middle Persian name for India, introduced during the Mughal Empire and used widely since. Its meaning has varied, referring to a region encompassing present-day northern India and Pakistan or to India in its near entirety.[75][79][80]

History

Main articles: History of India and History of the Republic of India

Ancient India

An illustration from an early-modern manuscript of the Sanskrit epic Ramayana, composed in story-telling fashion c. 400 BCE – c. 300 CE.[81]

By 55,000 years ago, the first modern humans, or Homo sapiens, had arrived on the Indian subcontinent from Africa, where they had earlier evolved.[27][28][29] The earliest known modern human remains in South Asia date to about 30,000 years ago.[27] After 6500 BCE, evidence for domestication of food crops and animals, construction of permanent structures, and storage of agricultural surplus appeared in Mehrgarh and other sites in what is now Balochistan, Pakistan.[82] These gradually developed into the Indus Valley Civilisation,[83][82] the first urban culture in South Asia,[84] which flourished during 2500–1900 BCE in what is now Pakistan and western India.[85] Centred around cities such as Mohenjo-daro, Harappa, Dholavira, and Kalibangan, and relying on varied forms of subsistence, the civilisation engaged robustly in crafts production and wide-ranging trade.[84]

During the period 2000–500 BCE, many regions of the subcontinent transitioned from the Chalcolithic cultures to the Iron Age ones.[86] The Vedas, the oldest scriptures associated with Hinduism,[87] were composed during this period,[88] and historians have analysed these to posit a Vedic culture in the Punjab region and the upper Gangetic Plain.[86] Most historians also consider this period to have encompassed several waves of Indo-Aryan migration into the subcontinent from the north-west.[87] The caste system, which created a hierarchy of priests, warriors, and free peasants, but which excluded indigenous peoples by labelling their occupations impure, arose during this period.[89] On the Deccan Plateau, archaeological evidence from this period suggests the existence of a chiefdom stage of political organisation.[86] In South India, a progression to sedentary life is indicated by the large number of megalithic monuments dating from this period,[90] as well as by nearby traces of agriculture, irrigation tanks, and craft traditions.[90]

Cave 26 of the rock-cut Ajanta Caves

In the late Vedic period, around the 6th century BCE, the small states and chiefdoms of the Ganges Plain and the north-western regions had consolidated into 16 major oligarchies and monarchies that were known as the mahajanapadas.[91][92] The emerging urbanisation gave rise to non-Vedic religious movements, two of which became independent religions. Jainism came into prominence during the life of its exemplar, Mahavira.[93] Buddhism, based on the teachings of Gautama Buddha, attracted followers from all social classes excepting the middle class; chronicling the life of the Buddha was central to the beginnings of recorded history in India.[94][95][96] In an age of increasing urban wealth, both religions held up renunciation as an ideal,[97] and both established long-lasting monastic traditions. Politically, by the 3rd century BCE, the kingdom of Magadha had annexed or reduced other states to emerge as the Mauryan Empire.[98] The empire was once thought to have controlled most of the subcontinent except the far south, but its core regions are now thought to have been separated by large autonomous areas.[99][100] The Mauryan kings are known as much for their empire-building and determined management of public life as for Ashoka's renunciation of militarism and far-flung advocacy of the Buddhist dhamma.[101][102]

The Sangam literature of the Tamil language reveals that, between 200 BCE and 200 CE, the southern peninsula was ruled by the Cheras, the Cholas, and the Pandyas, dynasties that traded extensively with the Roman Empire and with West and South-East Asia.[103][104] In North India, Hinduism asserted patriarchal control within the family, leading to increased subordination of women.[105][98] By the 4th and 5th centuries, the Gupta Empire had created a complex system of administration and taxation in the greater Ganges Plain; this system became a model for later Indian kingdoms.[106][107] Under the Guptas, a renewed Hinduism based on devotion, rather than the management of ritual, began to assert itself.[108] This renewal was reflected in a flowering of sculpture and architecture, which found patrons among an urban elite.[107] Classical Sanskrit literature flowered as well, and Indian science, astronomy, medicine, and mathematics made significant advances.[107]

Medieval India

Brihadeshwara temple, Thanjavur, completed in 1010 CE

The Qutub Minar, 73 m (240 ft) tall, completed by the Sultan of Delhi, Iltutmish

The Indian early medieval age, from 600 to 1200 CE, is defined by regional kingdoms and cultural diversity.[109] When Harsha of Kannauj, who ruled much of the Indo-Gangetic Plain from 606 to 647 CE, attempted to expand southwards, he was defeated by the Chalukya ruler of the Deccan.[110] When his successor attempted to expand eastwards, he was defeated by the Pala king of Bengal.[110] When the Chalukyas attempted to expand southwards, they were defeated by the Pallavas from farther south, who in turn were opposed by the Pandyas and the Cholas from still farther south.[110] No ruler of this period was able to create an empire and consistently control lands much beyond their core region.[109] During this time, pastoral peoples, whose land had been cleared to make way for the growing agricultural economy, were accommodated within caste society, as were new non-traditional ruling classes.[111] The caste system consequently began to show regional differences.[111]

In the 6th and 7th centuries, the first devotional hymns were created in the Tamil language.[112] They were imitated all over India and led to both the resurgence of Hinduism and the development of all modern languages of the subcontinent.[112] Indian royalty, big and small, and the temples they patronised drew citizens in great numbers to the capital cities, which became economic hubs as well.[113] Temple towns of various sizes began to appear everywhere as India underwent another urbanisation.[113] By the 8th and 9th centuries, the effects were felt in South-East Asia, as South Indian culture and political systems were exported to lands that became part of modern-day Myanmar, Thailand, Laos, Brunei, Cambodia, Vietnam, Philippines, Malaysia, and Indonesia.[114] Indian merchants, scholars, and sometimes armies were involved in this transmission; South-East Asians took the initiative as well, with many sojourning in Indian seminaries and translating Buddhist and Hindu texts into their languages.[114]

After the 10th century, Muslim Central Asian nomadic clans, using swift-horse cavalry and raising vast armies united by ethnicity and religion, repeatedly overran South Asia's north-western plains, leading eventually to the establishment of the Islamic Delhi Sultanate in 1206.[115] The sultanate was to control much of North India and to make many forays into South India. Although at first disruptive for the Indian elites, the sultanate largely left its vast non-Muslim subject population to its own laws and customs.[116][117] By repeatedly repulsing Mongol raiders in the 13th century, the sultanate saved India from the devastation visited on West and Central Asia, setting the scene for centuries of migration of fleeing soldiers, learned men, mystics, traders, artists, and artisans from that region into the subcontinent, thereby creating a syncretic Indo-Islamic culture in the north.[118][119] The sultanate's raiding and weakening of the regional kingdoms of South India paved the way for the indigenous Vijayanagara Empire.[120] Embracing a strong Shaivite tradition and building upon the military technology of the sultanate, the empire came to control much of peninsular India,[121] and was to influence South Indian society for long afterwards.[120]

Early modern India

In the early 16th century, northern India, then under mainly Muslim rulers,[122] fell again to the superior mobility and firepower of a new generation of Central Asian warriors.[123] The resulting Mughal Empire did not stamp out the local societies it came to rule. Instead, it balanced and pacified them through new administrative practices[124][125] and diverse and inclusive ruling elites,[126] leading to more systematic, centralised, and uniform rule.[127] Eschewing tribal bonds and Islamic identity, especially under Akbar, the Mughals united their far-flung realms through loyalty, expressed through a Persianised culture, to an emperor who had near-divine status.[126] The Mughal state's economic policies, deriving most revenues from agriculture[128] and mandating that taxes be paid in the well-regulated silver currency,[129] caused peasants and artisans to enter larger markets.[127] The relative peace maintained by the empire during much of the 17th century was a factor in India's economic expansion,[127] resulting in greater patronage of painting, literary forms, textiles, and architecture.[130] Newly coherent social groups in northern and western India, such as the Marathas, the Rajputs, and the Sikhs, gained military and governing ambitions during Mughal rule, which, through collaboration or adversity, gave them both recognition and military experience.[131] Expanding commerce during Mughal rule gave rise to new Indian commercial and political elites along the coasts of southern and eastern India.[131] As the empire disintegrated, many among these elites were able to seek and control their own affairs.[132]

A distant view of the Taj Mahal from the Agra Fort

A two mohur Company gold coin, issued in 1835, the obverse inscribed "William IV, King"

By the early 18th century, with the lines between commercial and political dominance being increasingly blurred, a number of European trading companies, including the English East India Company, had established coastal outposts.[133][134] The East India Company's control of the seas, greater resources, and more advanced military training and technology led it to increasingly assert its military strength and caused it to become attractive to a portion of the Indian elite; these factors were crucial in allowing the company to gain control over the Bengal region by 1765 and sideline the other European companies.[135][133][136][137] Its further access to the riches of Bengal and the subsequent increased strength and size of its army enabled it to annexe or subdue most of India by the 1820s.[138] India was then no longer exporting manufactured goods as it long had, but was instead supplying the British Empire with raw materials. Many historians consider this to be the onset of India's colonial period.[133] By this time, with its economic power severely curtailed by the British parliament and having effectively been made an arm of British administration, the company began more consciously to enter non-economic arenas, including education, social reform and culture.[139]

Modern India

Main article: History of the Republic of India

Historians consider India's modern age to have begun sometime between 1848 and 1885. The appointment in 1848 of Lord Dalhousie as Governor General of the East India Company set the stage for changes essential to a modern state. These included the consolidation and demarcation of sovereignty, the surveillance of the population, and the education of citizens. Technological changes—among them, railways, canals, and the telegraph—were introduced not long after their introduction in Europe.[140][141][142][143] However, disaffection with the company also grew during this time and set off the Indian Rebellion of 1857. Fed by diverse resentments and perceptions, including invasive British-style social reforms, harsh land taxes, and summary treatment of some rich landowners and princes, the rebellion rocked many regions of northern and central India and shook the foundations of Company rule.[144][145] Although the rebellion was suppressed by 1858, it led to the dissolution of the East India Company and the direct administration of India by the British government. Proclaiming a unitary state and a gradual but limited British-style parliamentary system, the new rulers also protected princes and landed gentry as a feudal safeguard against future unrest.[146][147] In the decades following, public life gradually emerged all over India, leading eventually to the founding of the Indian National Congress in 1885.[148][149][150][151]

The rush of technology and the commercialisation of agriculture in the second half of the 19th century was marked by economic setbacks and many small farmers became dependent on the whims of far-away markets.[152] There was an increase in the number of large-scale famines,[153] and, despite the risks of infrastructure development borne by Indian taxpayers, little industrial employment was generated for Indians.[154] There were also salutary effects: commercial cropping, especially in the newly canalled Punjab, led to increased food production for internal consumption.[155] The railway network provided critical famine relief,[156] notably reduced the cost of moving goods,[156] and helped nascent Indian-owned industry.[155]

1909 map of the British Indian Empire

Jawaharlal Nehru sharing a light moment with Mohandas Karamchand Gandhi, Mumbai, 6 July 1946

After World War I, in which approximately one million Indians served,[157] a new period began. It was marked by British reforms but also repressive legislation, by more strident Indian calls for self-rule, and by the beginnings of a nonviolent movement of non-co-operation, of which Mohandas Karamchand Gandhi would become the leader and enduring symbol.[158] During the 1930s, slow legislative reform was enacted by the British; the Indian National Congress won victories in the resulting elections.[159] The next decade was beset with crises: Indian participation in World War II, the Congress's final push for non-co-operation, and an upsurge of Muslim nationalism. All were capped by the advent of independence in 1947, but tempered by the partition of India into two states: India and Pakistan.[160]

Vital to India's self-image as an independent nation was its constitution, completed in 1950, which put in place a secular and democratic republic.[161] It has remained a democracy with civil liberties, an active supreme court, and a largely independent press.[dubious – discuss][162] Economic liberalisation, which began in the 1990s, has created a large urban middle class, transformed India into one of the world's fastest-growing economies,[163] and increased its geopolitical clout. Indian movies, music, and spiritual teachings play an increasing role in global culture.[162] Yet, India is also shaped by seemingly unyielding poverty, both rural and urban;[162] by religious and caste-related violence;[164] by Maoist-inspired Naxalite insurgencies;[165] and by separatism in Jammu and Kashmir and in Northeast India.[166] It has unresolved territorial disputes with China[167] and with Pakistan.[167] India's sustained democratic freedoms are unique among the world's newer nations; however, in spite of its recent economic successes, freedom from want for its disadvantaged population remains a goal yet to be achieved.[168]

Geography

Main article: Geography of India

India accounts for the bulk of the Indian subcontinent, lying atop the Indian tectonic plate, a part of the Indo-Australian Plate.[169] India's defining geological processes began 75 million years ago when the Indian Plate, then part of the southern supercontinent Gondwana, began a north-eastward drift caused by seafloor spreading to its southwest, and later, south and south-east.[169] Simultaneously, the vast Tethyan oceanic crust, to its northeast, began to subduct under the Eurasian Plate.[169] These dual processes, driven by convection in the Earth's mantle, both created the Indian Ocean and caused the Indian continental crust eventually to under-thrust Eurasia and to uplift the Himalayas.[169] Immediately south of the emerging Himalayas, plate movement created a vast crescent-shaped trough that rapidly filled with river-borne sediment[170] and now constitutes the Indo-Gangetic Plain.[171] The original Indian plate makes its first appearance above the sediment in the ancient Aravalli range, which extends from the Delhi Ridge in a southwesterly direction. To the west lies the Thar desert, the eastern spread of which is checked by the Aravallis.[172][173][174]

The Tungabhadra, with rocky outcrops, flows into the peninsular Krishna river.[175]

Fishing boats lashed together before a monsoon storm in a tidal creek in Anjarle village, Maharashtra.

The remaining Indian Plate survives as peninsular India, the oldest and geologically most stable part of India. It extends as far north as the Satpura and Vindhya ranges in central India. These parallel chains run from the Arabian Sea coast in Gujarat in the west to the coal-rich Chota Nagpur Plateau in Jharkhand in the east.[176] To the south, the remaining peninsular landmass, the Deccan Plateau, is flanked on the west and east by coastal ranges known as the Western and Eastern Ghats;[177] the plateau contains the country's oldest rock formations, some over one billion years old. Constituted in such fashion, India lies to the north of the equator between 6° 44′ and 35° 30′ north latitude[i] and 68° 7′ and 97° 25′ east longitude.[178]

India's coastline measures 7,517 kilometres (4,700 mi) in length; of this distance, 5,423 kilometres (3,400 mi) belong to peninsular India and 2,094 kilometres (1,300 mi) to the Andaman, Nicobar, and Lakshadweep island chains.[179] According to the Indian naval hydrographic charts, the mainland coastline consists of the following: 43% sandy beaches; 11% rocky shores, including cliffs; and 46% mudflats or marshy shores.[179]

Major Himalayan-origin rivers that substantially flow through India include the Ganges and the Brahmaputra, both of which drain into the Bay of Bengal.[180] Important tributaries of the Ganges include the Yamuna and the Kosi; the latter's extremely low gradient, caused by long-term silt deposition, leads to severe floods and course changes.[181][182] Major peninsular rivers, whose steeper gradients prevent their waters from flooding, include the Godavari, the Mahanadi, the Kaveri, and the Krishna, which also drain into the Bay of Bengal;[183] and the Narmada and the Tapti, which drain into the Arabian Sea.[184] Coastal features include the marshy Rann of Kutch of western India and the alluvial Sundarbans delta of eastern India; the latter is shared with Bangladesh.[185] India has two archipelagos: the Lakshadweep, coral atolls off India's south-western coast; and the Andaman and Nicobar Islands, a volcanic chain in the Andaman Sea.[186]

Indian climate is strongly influenced by the Himalayas and the Thar Desert, both of which drive the economically and culturally pivotal summer and winter monsoons.[187] The Himalayas prevent cold Central Asian katabatic winds from blowing in, keeping the bulk of the Indian subcontinent warmer than most locations at similar latitudes.[188][189] The Thar Desert plays a crucial role in attracting the moisture-laden south-west summer monsoon winds that, between June and October, provide the majority of India's rainfall.[187] Four major climatic groupings predominate in India: tropical wet, tropical dry, subtropical humid, and montane.[190]

Temperatures in India have risen by 0.7 °C (1.3 °F) between 1901 and 2018.[191] Climate change in India is often thought to be the cause. The retreat of Himalayan glaciers has adversely affected the flow rate of the major Himalayan rivers, including the Ganges and the Brahmaputra.[192] According to some current projections, the number and severity of droughts in India will have markedly increased by the end of the present century.[193]

Biodiversity

Main articles: Forestry in India and Wildlife of India

India has the majority of the world's wild tigers, approximately 3,000 in 2019.[194]

A Chital (Axis axis) stag attempts to browse in the Nagarhole National Park in a region covered by a moderately dense[j] forest.[195]

India is a megadiverse country, a term employed for 17 countries which display high biological diversity and contain many species exclusively indigenous, or endemic, to them.[196] India is a habitat for 8.6% of all mammal species, 13.7% of bird species, 7.9% of reptile species, 6% of amphibian species, 12.2% of fish species, and 6.0% of all flowering plant species.[197][198] Fully a third of Indian plant species are endemic.[199] India also contains four of the world's 34 biodiversity hotspots,[69] or regions that display significant habitat loss in the presence of high endemism.[k][200]

According to official statistics, India's forest cover is 713,789 km2 (275,595 sq mi), which is 21.71% of the country's total land area.[70] It can be subdivided further into broad categories of canopy density, or the proportion of the area of a forest covered by its tree canopy.[201] Very dense forest, whose canopy density is greater than 70%, occupies 3.02% of India's land area.[201][202] It predominates in the tropical moist forest of the Andaman Islands, the Western Ghats, and Northeast India.[195] Moderately dense forest, whose canopy density is between 40% and 70%, occupies 9.39% of India's land area.[201][202] It predominates in the temperate coniferous forest of the Himalayas, the moist deciduous sal forest of eastern India, and the dry deciduous teak forest of central and southern India.[195] Open forest, whose canopy density is between 10% and 40%, occupies 9.26% of India's land area.[201][202] India has two natural zones of thorn forest, one in the Deccan Plateau, immediately east of the Western Ghats, and the other in the western part of the Indo-Gangetic plain, now turned into rich agricultural land by irrigation, its features no longer visible.[203]

Among the Indian subcontinent's notable indigenous trees are the astringent Azadirachta indica, or neem, which is widely used in rural Indian herbal medicine,[204] and the luxuriant Ficus religiosa, or peepul,[205] which is displayed on the ancient seals of Mohenjo-daro,[206] and under which the Buddha is recorded in the Pali canon to have sought enlightenment.[207]

Many Indian species have descended from those of Gondwana, the southern supercontinent from which India separated more than 100 million years ago.[208] India's subsequent collision with Eurasia set off a mass exchange of species. However, volcanism and climatic changes later caused the extinction of many endemic Indian forms.[209] Still later, mammals entered India from Asia through two zoogeographical passes flanking the Himalayas.[195] This had the effect of lowering endemism among India's mammals, which stands at 12.6%, contrasting with 45.8% among reptiles and 55.8% among amphibians.[198]} Among endemics are the vulnerable[210] hooded leaf monkey[211] and the threatened[212] Beddome's toad[212][213] of the Western Ghats.

The last three Asiatic cheetahs (on record) in India were shot dead in Surguja district, Madhya Pradesh, Central India by Maharajah Ramanuj Pratap Singh Deo. The young males, all from the same litter, were sitting together when they were shot at night in 1948.

India contains 172 IUCN-designated threatened animal species, or 2.9% of endangered forms.[214] These include the endangered Bengal tiger and the Ganges river dolphin. Critically endangered species include: the gharial, a crocodilian; the great Indian bustard; and the Indian white-rumped vulture, which has become nearly extinct by having ingested the carrion of diclofenac-treated cattle.[215] Before they were extensively utilized for agriculture and cleared for human settlement, the thorn forests of Punjab were mingled at intervals with open grasslands that were grazed by large herds of blackbuck preyed on by the Asiatic cheetah; the blackbuck, no longer extant in Punjab, is now severely endangered in India, and the cheetah is extinct.[216] The pervasive and ecologically devastating human encroachment of recent decades has critically endangered Indian wildlife. In response, the system of national parks and protected areas, first established in 1935, was expanded substantially. In 1972, India enacted the Wildlife Protection Act[217] and Project Tiger to safeguard crucial wilderness; the Forest Conservation Act was enacted in 1980 and amendments added in 1988.[218] India hosts more than five hundred wildlife sanctuaries and thirteen biosphere reserves,[219] four of which are part of the World Network of Biosphere Reserves; twenty-five wetlands are registered under the Ramsar Convention.[220]

Politics and government

Politics

Main article: Politics of India

Social movements have long been a part of democracy in India. The picture shows a section of 25,000 landless people in the state of Madhya Pradesh listening to Rajagopal P. V. before their 350 km (220 mi) march, Janadesh 2007, from Gwalior to New Delhi to publicise their demand for further land reform in India.[221]

India is the world's most populous democracy.[222] A parliamentary republic with a multi-party system,[223] it has eight recognised national parties, including the Indian National Congress and the Bharatiya Janata Party (BJP), and more than 40 regional parties.[224] The Congress is considered centre-left in Indian political culture,[225] and the BJP right-wing.[226][227][228] For most of the period between 1950—when India first became a republic—and the late 1980s, the Congress held a majority in the parliament. Since then, however, it has increasingly shared the political stage with the BJP,[229] as well as with powerful regional parties which have often forced the creation of multi-party coalition governments at the centre.[230]

In the Republic of India's first three general elections, in 1951, 1957, and 1962, the Jawaharlal Nehru-led Congress won easy victories. On Nehru's death in 1964, Lal Bahadur Shastri briefly became prime minister; he was succeeded, after his own unexpected death in 1966, by Nehru's daughter Indira Gandhi, who went on to lead the Congress to election victories in 1967 and 1971. Following public discontent with the state of emergency she declared in 1975, the Congress was voted out of power in 1977; the then-new Janata Party, which had opposed the emergency, was voted in. Its government lasted just over two years. Voted back into power in 1980, the Congress saw a change in leadership in 1984, when Indira Gandhi was assassinated; she was succeeded by her son Rajiv Gandhi, who won an easy victory in the general elections later that year. The Congress was voted out again in 1989 when a National Front coalition, led by the newly formed Janata Dal in alliance with the Left Front, won the elections; that government too proved relatively short-lived, lasting just under two years.[231] Elections were held again in 1991; no party won an absolute majority. The Congress, as the largest single party, was able to form a minority government led by P. V. Narasimha Rao.[232]

At the Parliament of India in New Delhi, US president Barack Obama is shown here addressing the members of Parliament of both houses, the lower, Lok Sabha, and the upper, Rajya Sabha, in a joint session, 8 November 2010.

A two-year period of political turmoil followed the general election of 1996. Several short-lived alliances shared power at the centre. The BJP formed a government briefly in 1996; it was followed by two comparatively long-lasting United Front coalitions, which depended on external support. In 1998, the BJP was able to form a successful coalition, the National Democratic Alliance (NDA). Led by Atal Bihari Vajpayee, the NDA became the first non-Congress, coalition government to complete a five-year term.[233] Again in the 2004 Indian general elections, no party won an absolute majority, but the Congress emerged as the largest single party, forming another successful coalition: the United Progressive Alliance (UPA). It had the support of left-leaning parties and MPs who opposed the BJP. The UPA returned to power in the 2009 general election with increased numbers, and it no longer required external support from India's communist parties.[234] That year, Manmohan Singh became the first prime minister since Jawaharlal Nehru in 1957 and 1962 to be re-elected to a consecutive five-year term.[235] In the 2014 general election, the BJP became the first political party since 1984 to win a majority and govern without the support of other parties.[236] The incumbent prime minister is Narendra Modi, a former chief minister of Gujarat. On 20 July 2017, Ram Nath Kovind was elected India's 14th president and took the oath of office on 25 July 2017.[237]

Government

Main articles: Government of India and Constitution of India

Rashtrapati Bhavan, the official residence of the President of India, was designed by British architects Edwin Lutyens and Herbert Baker for the Viceroy of India, and constructed between 1911 and 1931 during the British Raj.[238]

India is a federation with a parliamentary system governed under the Constitution of India—the country's supreme legal document. It is a constitutional republic and representative democracy, in which "majority rule is tempered by minority rights protected by law". Federalism in India defines the power distribution between the union and the states. The Constitution of India, which came into effect on 26 January 1950,[239] originally stated India to be a "sovereign, democratic republic;" this characterisation was amended in 1971 to "a sovereign, socialist, secular, democratic republic".[240] India's form of government, traditionally described as "quasi-federal" with a strong centre and weak states,[241] has grown increasingly federal since the late 1990s as a result of political, economic, and social changes.[242][243]

National symbols[1]

FlagTiranga (Tricolour)

EmblemSarnath Lion Capital

AnthemJana Gana Mana

Song"Vande Mataram"

LanguageNone[9][10][11]

Currency? (Indian rupee)

CalendarSaka

Animal

Bengal tiger

River dolphin

Indian peafowl

FlowerLotus

FruitMango

TreeBanyan

RiverGanges

The Government of India comprises three branches:[244]

Executive: The President of India is the ceremonial head of state,[245] who is elected indirectly for a five-year term by an electoral college comprising members of national and state legislatures.[246][247] The Prime Minister of India is the head of government and exercises most executive power.[248] Appointed by the president,[249] the prime minister is by convention supported by the party or political alliance having a majority of seats in the lower house of parliament.[248] The executive of the Indian government consists of the president, the vice president, and the Union Council of Ministers—with the cabinet being its executive committee—headed by the prime minister. Any minister holding a portfolio must be a member of one of the houses of parliament.[245] In the Indian parliamentary system, the executive is subordinate to the legislature; the prime minister and their council are directly responsible to the lower house of the parliament. Civil servants act as permanent executives and all decisions of the executive are implemented by them.[250]

Legislature: The legislature of India is the bicameral parliament. Operating under a Westminster-style parliamentary system, it comprises an upper house called the Rajya Sabha (Council of States) and a lower house called the Lok Sabha (House of the People).[251] The Rajya Sabha is a permanent body of 245 members who serve staggered six-year terms.[252] Most are elected indirectly by the state and union territorial legislatures in numbers proportional to their state's share of the national population.[249] All but two of the Lok Sabha's 545 members are elected directly by popular vote; they represent single-member constituencies for five-year terms.[253] Two seats of parliament, reserved for Anglo-Indian in the article 331, have been scrapped.[254][255]

Judiciary: India has a three-tier unitary independent judiciary[256] comprising the supreme court, headed by the Chief Justice of India, 25 high courts, and a large number of trial courts.[256] The supreme court has original jurisdiction over cases involving fundamental rights and over disputes between states and the centre and has appellate jurisdiction over the high courts.[257] It has the power to both strike down union or state laws which contravene the constitution,[258] and invalidate any government action it deems unconstitutional.[259]

Administrative divisions

Main article: Administrative divisions of India

See also: Political integration of India

India is a federal union comprising 28 states and 8 union territories.[16] All states, as well as the union territories of Jammu and Kashmir, Puducherry and the National Capital Territory of Delhi, have elected legislatures and governments following the Westminster system of governance. The remaining five union territories are directly ruled by the central government through appointed administrators. In 1956, under the States Reorganisation Act, states were reorganised on a linguistic basis.[260] There are over a quarter of a million local government bodies at city, town, block, district and village levels.[261]

A clickable map of the 28 states and 8 union territories of India

States

Andhra Pradesh

Arunachal Pradesh

Assam

Bihar

Chhattisgarh

Goa

Gujarat

Haryana

Himachal Pradesh

Jharkhand

Karnataka

Kerala

Madhya Pradesh

Maharashtra

Manipur

Meghalaya
Mizoram
Nagaland
Odisha
Punjab
Rajasthan
Sikkim
Tamil Nadu
Telangana
Tripura
Uttar Pradesh
Uttarakhand
West Bengal
Union territories
Andaman and Nicobar Islands
Chandigarh
Dadra and Nagar Haveli and Daman and Diu
Jammu and Kashmir
Ladakh

CHAPTER TWO

Indian

Indian cultural history spans more than 4,500 years.[368] During the Vedic period (c. 1700 BCE – c. 500 BCE), the foundations of Hindu philosophy, mythology, theology and literature were laid, and many beliefs and practices which still exist today, such as dhárma, kárma, yóga, and mokṣa, were established.[74] India is notable for its religious diversity, with Hinduism, Buddhism, Sikhism, Islam, Christianity, and Jainism among the nation's major religions.[369] The predominant religion, Hinduism, has been shaped by various historical schools of thought, including those of the Upanishads,[370] the Yoga Sutras, the Bhakti movement,[369] and by Buddhist philosophy.[371]

Visual art

Main article: Indian art

India has a very ancient tradition of art, which has exchanged many influences with the rest of Eurasia, especially in the first millennium, when Buddhist art spread with Indian religions to Central, East and South-East Asia, the last also greatly influenced by Hindu art.[372] Thousands of seals from the Indus Valley Civilization of the third millennium BCE have been found, usually carved with animals, but a few with human figures. The "Pashupati" seal, excavated in Mohenjo-daro, Pakistan, in 1928–29, is the best known.[373][374] After this there is a long period with virtually nothing surviving.[374][375] Almost all surviving ancient Indian art thereafter is in various forms of religious sculpture in durable materials, or coins. There was probably originally far more in wood, which is lost. In north India Mauryan art is the first imperial movement.[376][377][378] In the first millennium CE, Buddhist art spread with Indian religions to Central, East and South-East Asia, the last also greatly influenced by Hindu art.[379] Over the following centuries a distinctly Indian style of sculpting the human figure developed, with less interest in articulating precise anatomy than ancient Greek sculpture but showing smoothly-flowing forms expressing prana ("breath" or life-force).[380][381] This is often complicated by the need to give figures multiple arms or heads, or represent different genders on the left and right of figures, as with the Ardhanarishvara form of Shiva and Parvati.[382][383]

Most of the earliest large sculpture is Buddhist, either excavated from Buddhist stupas such as Sanchi, Sarnath and Amaravati,[384] or is rock-cut reliefs at sites such as Ajanta, Karla and Ellora. Hindu and Jain sites appear rather later.[385][386] In spite of this complex mixture of religious traditions, generally, the prevailing artistic style at any time and place has been shared by the major religious groups, and sculptors probably usually served all communities.[387] Gupta art, at its peak c. 300 CE – c. 500 CE, is often regarded as a classical period whose influence lingered for many centuries after; it saw a new dominance of Hindu sculpture, as at the Elephanta Caves.[388][389] Across the north, this became rather stiff and formulaic after c. 800 CE, though rich with finely carved detail in the surrounds of statues.[390] But in the South, under the Pallava and Chola dynasties, sculpture in both stone and bronze had a sustained period of great achievement; the large bronzes with Shiva as Nataraja have become an iconic symbol of India.[391][392]

Ancient painting has only survived at a few sites, of which the crowded scenes of court life in the Ajanta Caves are by far the most important, but it was evidently highly developed, and is mentioned as a courtly accomplishment in Gupta times.[393][394] Painted manuscripts of religious texts survive from Eastern India about the 10th century onwards, most of the earliest being Buddhist and later Jain. No doubt the style of these was used in larger paintings.[395] The Persian-derived Deccan painting, starting just before the Mughal miniature, between them give the first large body of secular painting, with an emphasis on portraits, and the recording of princely pleasures and wars.[396][397] The style spread to Hindu courts, especially among the Rajputs, and developed a variety of styles, with the smaller courts often the most innovative, with figures such as Nihâl Chand and Nainsukh.[398][399] As a market developed among European residents, it was supplied by Company painting by Indian artists with considerable Western influence.[400][401] In the 19th century, cheap Kalighat paintings of gods and everyday life, done on paper, were urban folk art from Calcutta, which later saw the Bengal School of Art, reflecting the art colleges founded by the British, the first movement in modern Indian painting.[402][403]

Bhutesvara Yakshis, Buddhist reliefs from Mathura, 2nd century CE

Gupta terracotta relief, Krishna Killing the Horse Demon Keshi, 5th century

Elephanta Caves, triple-bust (trimurti) of Shiva, 18 feet (5.5 m) tall, c. 550

Chola bronze of Shiva as Nataraja ("Lord of Dance"), Tamil Nadu, 10th or 11th century.

Jahangir Receives Prince Khurram at Ajmer on His Return from the Mewar Campaign, Balchand, c. 1635

Krishna Fluting to the Milkmaids, Kangra painting, 1775–1785

Architecture

Main article: Architecture of India

The Taj Mahal from across the Yamuna river showing two outlying red sandstone buildings, a mosque on the right (west) and a jawab (response) thought to have been built for architectural balance.

Much of Indian architecture, including the Taj Mahal, other works of Indo-Islamic Mughal architecture, and South Indian architecture, blends ancient local traditions with imported styles.[404] Vernacular architecture is also regional in its flavours. Vastu shastra, literally "science of construction" or "architecture" and ascribed to Mamuni Mayan,[405] explores how the laws of nature affect human dwellings;[406] it employs precise geometry and directional alignments to reflect perceived cosmic constructs.[407] As applied in Hindu temple architecture, it is influenced by the Shilpa Shastras, a series of foundational texts whose basic mythological form is the Vastu-Purusha mandala, a square that embodied the "absolute".[408] The Taj Mahal, built in Agra between 1631 and 1648 by orders of Mughal emperor Shah Jahan in memory of his wife, has been described in the UNESCO World Heritage List as "the jewel of Muslim art in India and one of the universally admired masterpieces of the world's heritage".[409] Indo-Saracenic Revival architecture, developed by the British in the late 19th century, drew on Indo-Islamic architecture.[410]

Literature

Main article: Indian literature

The earliest literature in India, composed between 1500 BCE and 1200 CE, was in the Sanskrit language.[411] Major works of Sanskrit literature include the Rigveda (c. 1500 BCE – c. 1200 BCE), the epics: Mahābhārata (c. 400 BCE – c. 400 CE) and the Ramayana (c. 300 BCE and later); Abhijñānaśākuntalam (The Recognition of Śakuntalā, and other dramas of Kālidāsa (c. 5th century CE) and Mahākāvya poetry.[412][413][414] In Tamil literature, the Sangam literature (c. 600 BCE – c. 300 BCE) consisting of 2,381 poems, composed by 473 poets, is the earliest work.[415][416][417][418] From the 14th to the 18th centuries, India's literary traditions went through a period of drastic change because of the emergence of devotional poets like Kabīr, Tulsīdās, and Guru Nānak. This period was characterised by a varied and wide spectrum of thought and expression; as a consequence, medieval Indian literary works differed significantly from classical traditions.[419] In the 19th century, Indian writers took a new interest in social questions and psychological descriptions. In the 20th century, Indian literature was influenced by the works of the Bengali poet, author and philosopher Rabindranath Tagore,[420] who was a recipient of the Nobel Prize in Literature.

Performing arts and media

Main articles: Music of India, Dance in India, Cinema of India, and Television in India

India's National Academy of Performance Arts has recognised eight Indian dance styles to be classical. One such is Kuchipudi shown here.

Indian music ranges over various traditions and regional styles. Classical music encompasses two genres and their various folk offshoots: the northern Hindustani and southern Carnatic schools.[421] Regionalised popular forms include filmi and folk music; the syncretic tradition of the bauls is a well-known form of the latter. Indian dance also features diverse folk and classical forms. Among the better-known folk dances are: the bhangra of Punjab, the bihu of Assam, the Jhumair and chhau of Jharkhand, Odisha and West Bengal, garba and dandiya of Gujarat, ghoomar of Rajasthan, and the lavani of Maharashtra. Eight dance forms, many with narrative forms and mythological elements, have been accorded classical dance status by India's National Academy of Music, Dance, and Drama. These are: bharatanatyam of the state of Tamil Nadu, kathak of Uttar Pradesh, kathakali and mohiniyattam of Kerala, kuchipudi of Andhra Pradesh, manipuri of Manipur, odissi of Odisha, and the sattriya of Assam.[422]

Theatre in India melds music, dance, and improvised or written dialogue.[423] Often based on Hindu mythology, but also borrowing from medieval romances or social and political events, Indian theatre includes: the bhavai of Gujarat, the jatra of West Bengal, the nautanki and ramlila of North India, tamasha of Maharashtra, burrakatha of Andhra Pradesh and Telangana, terukkuttu of Tamil Nadu, and the yakshagana of Karnataka.[424] India has a theatre training institute the National School of Drama (NSD) that is situated at New Delhi It is an autonomous organisation under the Ministry of Culture, Government of India.[425] The Indian film industry produces the world's most-watched cinema.[426] Established regional cinematic traditions exist in the Assamese, Bengali, Bhojpuri, Hindi, Kannada, Malayalam, Punjabi, Gujarati, Marathi, Odia, Tamil, and Telugu languages.[427] The Hindi language film industry (Bollywood) is the largest sector representing 43% of box office revenue, followed by the South Indian Telugu and Tamil film industries which represent 36% combined.[428]

Television broadcasting began in India in 1959 as a state-run medium of communication and expanded slowly for more than two decades.[429][430] The state monopoly on television broadcast ended in the 1990s. Since then, satellite channels have increasingly shaped the popular culture of Indian society.[431] Today, television is the most penetrative media in India; industry estimates indicate that as of 2012 there are over 554 million TV consumers, 462 million with satellite or cable connections compared to other forms of mass media such as the press (350 million), radio (156 million) or internet (37 million).[432]

Society

Main article: Culture of India

Muslims offer namaz at a mosque in Srinagar, Jammu and Kashmir.

Traditional Indian society is sometimes defined by social hierarchy. The Indian caste system embodies much of the social stratification and many of the social restrictions found on the Indian subcontinent. Social classes are defined by thousands of endogamous hereditary groups, often termed as jātis, or "castes".[433] India declared untouchability to be illegal[434] in 1947 and has since enacted other anti-discriminatory laws and social welfare initiatives.

Family values are important in the Indian tradition, and multi-generational patrilineal joint families have been the norm in India, though nuclear families are becoming common in urban areas.[435] An overwhelming majority of Indians, with their consent, have their marriages arranged by their parents or other family elders.[436] Marriage is thought to be for life,[436] and the divorce rate is extremely low,[437] with less than one in a thousand marriages ending in divorce.[438] Child marriages are common, especially in rural areas; many women wed before reaching 18, which is their legal marriageable age.[439] Female infanticide in India, and lately female foeticide, have created skewed gender ratios; the number of missing women in the country quadrupled from 15 million to 63 million in the 50-year period ending in 2014, faster than the population growth during the same period, and constituting 20 percent of India's female electorate.[440] Accord to an Indian government study, an additional 21 million girls are unwanted and do not receive adequate care.[441] Despite a government ban on sex-selective foeticide, the practice remains commonplace in India, the result of a preference for boys in a patriarchal society.[442] The payment of dowry, although illegal, remains widespread across class lines.[443] Deaths resulting from dowry, mostly from bride burning, are on the rise, despite stringent anti-dowry laws.[444]

Many Indian festivals are religious in origin. The best known include: Diwali, Ganesh Chaturthi, Thai Pongal, Holi, Durga Puja, Eid ul-Fitr, Bakr-Id, Christmas, and Vaisakhi.[445][446]

Education

Main articles: Education in India, Literacy in India, and History of education in the Indian subcontinent

Children awaiting school lunch in Rayka (also Raika), a village in rural Gujarat. The salutation Jai Bhim written on the blackboard honours the jurist, social reformer, and Dalit leader B. R. Ambedkar.

In the 2011 census, about 73% of the population was literate, with 81% for men and 65% for women. This compares to 1981 when the respective rates were 41%, 53% and 29%. In 1951 the rates were 18%, 27% and 9%. In 1921 the rates 7%, 12% and 2%. In 1891 they were 5%, 9% and 1%,[447][448] According to Latika Chaudhary, in 1911 there were under three primary schools for every ten villages. Statistically, more caste and religious diversity reduced private spending. Primary schools taught literacy, so local diversity limited its growth.[449]

The education system of India is the world's second-largest.[450] India has over 900 universities, 40,000 colleges[451] and 1.5 million schools.[452] In India's higher education system, a significant number of seats are reserved under affirmative action policies for the historically disadvantaged. In recent decades India's improved education system is often cited as one of the main contributors to its economic development.[453][454]

Clothing

Main article: Clothing in India

Women in sari at an adult literacy class in Tamil Nadu

A man in dhoti and wearing a woollen shawl, in Varanasi

From ancient times until the advent of the modern, the most widely worn traditional dress in India was draped.[455] For women it took the form of a sari, a single piece of cloth many yards long.[455] The sari was traditionally wrapped around the lower body and the shoulder.[455] In its modern form, it is combined with an underskirt, or Indian petticoat, and tucked in the waist band for more secure fastening. It is also commonly worn with an Indian blouse, or choli, which serves as the primary upper-body garment, the sari's end—passing over the shoulder—serving to cover the midriff and obscure the upper body's contours.[455] For men, a similar but shorter length of cloth, the dhoti, has served as a lower-body garment.[456]

Women (from left to right) in churidars and kameez (with back to the camera), jeans and sweater, and pink Shalwar kameez;

The use of stitched clothes became widespread after Muslim rule was established at first by the Delhi sultanate (ca 1300 CE) and then continued by the Mughal Empire (ca 1525 CE).[457] Among the garments introduced during this time and still commonly worn are: the shalwars and pyjamas, both styles of trousers, and the tunics kurta and kameez.[457] In southern India, the traditional draped garments were to see much longer continuous use.[457]

Shalwars are atypically wide at the waist but narrow to a cuffed bottom. They are held up by a drawstring, which causes them to become pleated around the waist.[458] The pants can be wide and baggy, or they can be cut quite narrow, on the bias, in which case they are called churidars. When they are ordinarily wide at the waist and their bottoms are hemmed but not cuffed, they are called pyjamas. The kameez is a long shirt or tunic,[459] its side seams left open below the waist-line.[460] The kurta is traditionally collarless and made of cotton or silk; it is worn plain or with embroidered decoration, such as chikan; and typically falls to either just above or just below the wearer's knees.[461]

In the last 50 years, fashions have changed a great deal in India. Increasingly, in urban northern India, the sari is no longer the apparel of everyday wear, though they remain popular on formal occasions.[462] The traditional shalwar kameez is rarely worn by younger urban women, who favour churidars or jeans.[462] In white-collar office settings, ubiquitous air conditioning allows men to wear sports jackets year-round.[462] For weddings and formal occasions, men in the middle- and upper classes often wear bandgala, or short Nehru jackets, with pants, with the groom and his groomsmen sporting sherwanis and churidars.[462] The dhoti, once the universal garment of Hindu males, the wearing of which in the homespun and handwoven khadi allowed Gandhi to bring Indian nationalism to the millions,[463] is seldom seen in the cities.[462]

Cuisine

Main article: Indian cuisine

South Indian vegetarian thali, or platter

Railway mutton curry from Odisha

The foundation of a typical Indian meal is a cereal cooked in a plain fashion and complemented with flavourful savoury dishes.[464] The cooked cereal could be steamed rice; chapati, a thin unleavened bread made from wheat flour, or occasionally cornmeal, and griddle-cooked dry;[465] the idli, a steamed breakfast cake, or dosa, a griddled pancake, both leavened and made from a batter of rice- and gram meal.[466] The savoury dishes might include lentils, pulses and vegetables commonly spiced with ginger and garlic, but also with a combination of spices that may include coriander, cumin, turmeric, cinnamon, cardamon and others as informed by culinary conventions.[464] They might also include poultry, fish, or meat dishes. In some instances, the ingredients might be mixed during the process of cooking.[467]

A platter, or thali, used for eating usually has a central place reserved for the cooked cereal, and peripheral ones for the flavourful accompaniments, which are often served in small bowls. The cereal and its accompaniments are eaten simultaneously rather than a piecemeal manner. This is accomplished by mixing—for example of rice and lentils—or folding, wrapping, scooping or dipping—such as chapati and cooked vegetables or lentils.[464]

0:14

A tandoor chef in the Turkman Gate, Old Delhi, makes Khameeri roti (a Muslim-influenced style of leavened bread).[468]

India has distinctive vegetarian cuisines, each a feature of the geographical and cultural histories of its adherents.[469] The appearance of ahimsa, or the avoidance of violence toward all forms of life in many religious orders early in Indian history, especially Upanishadic Hinduism, Buddhism and Jainism, is thought to have contributed to the predominance of vegetarianism among a large segment of India's Hindu population, especially in southern India, Gujarat, the Hindi-speaking belt of north-central India, as well as among Jains.[469] Although meat is eaten widely in India, the proportional consumption of meat in the overall diet is low.[470] Unlike China, which has increased its per capita meat consumption substantially in its years of increased economic growth, in India the strong dietary traditions have contributed to dairy, rather than meat, becoming the preferred form of animal protein consumption.[471]

The most significant import of cooking techniques into India during the last millennium occurred during the Mughal Empire. Dishes such as the pilaf,[472] developed in the Abbasid caliphate,[473] and cooking techniques such as the marinating of meat in yogurt, spread into northern India from regions to its northwest.[474] To the simple yogurt marinade of Persia, onions, garlic, almonds, and spices began to be added in India.[474] Rice was partially cooked and layered alternately with the sauteed meat, the pot sealed tightly, and slow cooked according to another Persian cooking technique, to produce what has today become the Indian biryani,[474] a feature of festive dining in many parts of India.[475] In the food served in Indian restaurants worldwide the diversity of Indian food has been partially concealed by the dominance of Punjabi cuisine. The popularity of tandoori chicken—cooked in the tandoor oven, which had traditionally been used for baking bread in the rural Punjab and the Delhi region, especially among Muslims, but which is originally from Central Asia—dates to the 1950s, and was caused in large part by an entrepreneurial response among people from the Punjab who had been displaced by the 1947 partition of India.[469]

Sports and recreation

Main article: Sport in India

Girls play hopscotch in Jaora, Madhya Pradesh. Hopscotch has been commonly played by girls in rural India.[476]

Several traditional indigenous sports such as kabaddi, kho kho, pehlwani and gilli-danda, and also martial arts, such as Kalarippayattu and marma adi remain popular. Chess is commonly held to have originated in India as chaturaṅga;[477] There has been a rise in the number of Indian grandmasters.[478] Viswanathan Anand became the undisputed Chess World Champion in 2007 and held the status until 2013.[479] Parcheesi is derived from

Pachisi another traditional Indian pastime, which in early modern times was played on a giant marble court by Mughal emperor Akbar the Great.[480]

Cricket is the most popular sport in India.[481] Major domestic competitions include the Indian Premier League, which is the most-watched cricket league in the world and ranks sixth among all sports leagues.[482] Other professional leagues include the Indian Super League (football) and the pro Kabaddi league.[483][484][485]

Indian cricketer Sachin Tendulkar about to score a record 14,000 runs in test cricket while playing against Australia in Bangalore, 2010.

India has won two ODI Cricket world cups, the 1983 edition and the 2011 edition and has eight field hockey gold medals in the summer olympics[486] The improved results garnered by the Indian Davis Cup team and other Indian tennis players in the early 2010s have made tennis increasingly popular in the country.[487] India has a comparatively strong presence in shooting sports, and has won several medals at the Olympics, the World Shooting Championships, and the Commonwealth Games.[488][489] Other sports in which Indians have succeeded internationally include badminton[490] (Saina Nehwal and P. V. Sindhu are two of the top-ranked female badminton players in the world), boxing,[491] and wrestling.[492] Football is popular in West Bengal, Goa, Tamil Nadu, Kerala, and the north-eastern states.[493] India has hosted or co-hosted several international sporting events: the 1951 and 1982 Asian Games; the 1987, 1996, and 2011 Cricket World Cup tournaments; the 2003 Afro-Asian Games; the 2006 ICC Champions Trophy; the 2009 World Badminton Championships; the 2010 Hockey World Cup; the 2010 Commonwealth Games; and the 2017 FIFA

U-17 World Cup. Major international sporting events held annually in India include the Maharashtra Open, the Mumbai Marathon, the Delhi Half Marathon, and the Indian Masters. The first Formula 1 Indian Grand Prix featured in late 2011 but has been discontinued from the F1 season calendar since 2014.[494] India has traditionally been the dominant country at the South Asian Games. An example of this dominance is the basketball competition where the Indian team won three out of four tournaments to date.[495]

See also

Culture

In the 1950s, India strongly supported decolonisation in Africa and Asia and played a leading role in the Non-Aligned Movement.[263] After initially cordial relations with neighbouring China, India went to war with China in 1962, and was widely thought to have been humiliated.[264] India has had tense relations with neighbouring Pakistan; the two nations have gone to war four times: in 1947, 1965, 1971, and 1999. Three of these wars were fought over the disputed territory of Kashmir, while the fourth, the 1971 war, followed from India's support for the independence of Bangladesh.[265] In the late 1980s, the Indian military twice intervened abroad at the invitation of the host country: a peace-keeping operation in Sri Lanka between 1987 and 1990; and an armed intervention to prevent a 1988 coup d'état attempt in the Maldives. After the 1965 war with Pakistan, India began to pursue close military and economic ties with the Soviet Union; by the late 1960s, the Soviet Union was its largest arms supplier.[266]

Aside from ongoing its special relationship with Russia,[267] India has wide-ranging defence relations with Israel and France. In recent years, it has played key roles in the South Asian Association for Regional Cooperation and the World Trade Organization. The nation has provided 100,000 military and police personnel to serve in 35 UN peacekeeping operations across four continents. It participates in the East Asia Summit, the G8+5, and other multilateral forums.[268] India has close economic ties with countries in South America,[269] Asia, and Africa; it pursues a "Look East" policy that seeks to strengthen partnerships with the ASEAN nations, Japan, and South Korea that revolve around many issues, but especially those involving economic investment and regional security.[270][271]

The Indian Air Force contingent marching at the 221st Bastille Day military parade in Paris, on 14 July 2009. The parade at which India was the foreign guest was led by the India's oldest regiment, the Maratha Light Infantry, founded in 1768.[272]

China's nuclear test of 1964, as well as its repeated threats to intervene in support of Pakistan in the 1965 war, convinced India to develop nuclear weapons.[273] India conducted its first nuclear weapons test in 1974 and carried out additional underground testing in 1998. Despite criticism and military sanctions, India has signed neither the Comprehensive Nuclear-Test-Ban Treaty nor the Nuclear Non-Proliferation Treaty, considering both to be flawed and discriminatory.[274] India maintains a "no first use" nuclear policy and is developing a nuclear triad capability as a part of its "Minimum Credible Deterrence" doctrine.[275][276] It is developing a ballistic missile defence shield and, a fifth-generation fighter jet.[277][278] Other indigenous military projects involve the design and implementation of Vikrant-class aircraft carriers and Arihant-class nuclear submarines.[279]

Since the end of the Cold War, India has increased its economic, strategic, and military co-operation with the United States and the European Union.[280] In 2008, a civilian nuclear agreement was signed between India and the United States. Although India possessed nuclear weapons at the time and was not a party to the Nuclear Non-Proliferation Treaty, it received waivers from the International Atomic Energy Agency and the Nuclear Suppliers Group, ending earlier restrictions on India's nuclear technology and commerce. As a consequence, India became the sixth de facto nuclear weapons state.[281] India subsequently signed co-operation agreements involving civilian nuclear energy with Russia,[282] France,[283] the United Kingdom,[284] and Canada.[285]

Prime Minister Narendra Modi of India (left, background) in talks with President Enrique Peña Nieto of Mexico during a visit to Mexico, 2016

The President of India is the supreme commander of the nation's armed forces; with 1.45 million active troops, they compose the world's second-largest military. It comprises the Indian Army, the Indian Navy, the Indian Air Force, and the Indian Coast Guard.[286] The official Indian defence budget for 2011 was US$36.03 billion, or 1.83% of GDP.[287] Defence expenditure was pegged at US$70.12 billion for fiscal year 2022–23 and, increased 9.8% than previous fiscal year.[288][289] India is the world's second largest arms importer; between 2016 and 2020, it accounted for 9.5% of the total global arms imports.[290] Much of the military expenditure was focused on defence against Pakistan and countering growing Chinese influence in the Indian Ocean.[291] In May 2017, the Indian Space Research Organisation launched the South Asia Satellite, a gift from India to its neighbouring SAARC countries.[292]

In October 2018, India signed a US$5.43 billion (over ?400 billion) agreement with Russia to procure four S-400 Triumf surface-to-air missile defence systems, Russia's most advanced long-range missile defence system.[293]

Economy

Main article: Economy of India

A farmer in northwestern Karnataka ploughs his field with a tractor even as another in a field beyond does the same with a pair of oxen. In 2019, 43% of India's total workforce was employed in agriculture.[294]

India is the world's largest producer of milk, with the largest population of cattle. In 2018, nearly 80% of India's milk was sourced from small farms with herd size between one and two, the milk harvested by hand milking.[296]

Women tend to a recently planted rice field in Junagadh district in Gujarat. 55% of India's female workforce was employed in agriculture in 2019.[295]

According to the International Monetary Fund (IMF), the Indian economy in 2021 was nominally worth $3.04 trillion; it is the sixth-largest economy by market exchange rates, and is around $10.219 trillion, the third-largest by purchasing power parity (PPP).[297] With its average annual GDP growth rate of 5.8% over the past two decades, and reaching 6.1% during 2011–2012,[298] India is one of the world's fastest-growing economies.[299] However, the country ranks 139th in the world in nominal GDP per capita and 118th in GDP per capita at PPP.[300] Until 1991, all Indian governments followed protectionist policies that were influenced by socialist economics. Widespread state intervention and regulation largely walled the economy off from the outside world. An acute balance of payments crisis in 1991 forced the nation to liberalise its economy;[301] since then it has moved slowly towards a free-market system[302][303] by emphasising both foreign trade and direct investment inflows.[304] India has been a member of World Trade Organization since 1 January 1995.[305]

The 522-million-worker Indian labour force is the world's second-largest, as of 2017.[286] The service sector makes up 55.6% of GDP, the industrial sector 26.3% and the agricultural sector 18.1%. India's foreign exchange remittances of US$87 billion in 2021, highest in the world, were contributed to its economy by 32 million Indians working in foreign countries.[306] Major agricultural products include: rice, wheat, oilseed, cotton, jute, tea, sugarcane, and potatoes.[16] Major industries include: textiles, telecommunications, chemicals, pharmaceuticals, biotechnology, food processing, steel, transport equipment, cement, mining, petroleum, machinery, and software.[16] In 2006, the share of external trade in India's GDP stood at 24%, up from 6% in 1985.[302] In 2008, India's share of world trade was 1.68%;[307] In 2011, India was the world's tenth-largest importer and the nineteenth-largest exporter.[308] Major exports include: petroleum products, textile goods, jewellery, software, engineering goods, chemicals, and manufactured leather goods.[16] Major imports include: crude oil, machinery, gems, fertiliser, and chemicals.[16] Between 2001 and 2011, the contribution of petrochemical and engineering goods to total exports grew from 14% to 42%.[309] India was the world's second largest textile exporter after China in the 2013 calendar year.[310]

Averaging an economic growth rate of 7.5% for several years prior to 2007,[302] India has more than doubled its hourly wage rates during the first decade of the 21st century.[311] Some 431 million Indians have left poverty since 1985; India's middle classes are projected to number around 580 million by 2030.[312] Though ranking 51st in global competitiveness, as of 2010, India ranks 17th in financial market sophistication, 24th in the banking sector, 44th in business sophistication, and 39th in innovation, ahead of several advanced economies.[313] With seven of the world's top 15 information technology outsourcing companies based in India, as of 2009, the country is viewed as the second-most favourable outsourcing destination after the United States.[314] India was ranked 46th in the Global Innovation Index in 2021, it has increased its ranking considerably since 2015, where it was 81st.[315][316][317][318] India's consumer market, the world's eleventh-largest, is expected to become fifth-largest by 2030.[312]

Driven by growth, India's nominal GDP per capita increased steadily from US$308 in 1991, when economic liberalisation began, to US$1,380 in 2010, to an estimated US$1,730 in 2016. It is expected to grow to US$2,313 by 2022.[21] However, it has remained lower than those of other Asian developing countries such as Indonesia, Malaysia, Philippines, Sri Lanka, and Thailand, and is expected to remain so in the near future.

A panorama of Bangalore, the centre of India's software development economy. In the 1980s, when the first multinational corporations began to set up centres in India, they chose Bangalore because of the large pool of skilled graduates in the area, in turn due to the many science and engineering colleges in the surrounding region.[319]

According to a 2011 PricewaterhouseCoopers (PwC) report, India's GDP at purchasing power parity could overtake that of the United States by 2045.[320] During the next four decades, Indian GDP is expected to grow at an annualised average of 8%, making it potentially the world's fastest-growing major economy until 2050.[320] The report highlights key growth factors: a young and rapidly growing working-age population; growth in the manufacturing sector because of rising education and engineering skill levels; and sustained growth of the consumer market driven by a rapidly growing middle-class.[320] The World Bank cautions that, for India to achieve its economic potential, it must continue to focus on public sector reform, transport infrastructure, agricultural and rural development, removal of labour regulations, education, energy security, and public health and nutrition.[321]

According to the Worldwide Cost of Living Report 2017 released by the Economist Intelligence Unit (EIU) which was created by comparing more than 400 individual prices across 160 products and services, four of the cheapest cities were in India: Bangalore (3rd), Mumbai (5th), Chennai (5th) and New Delhi (8th).[322]

Industries

A tea garden in Sikkim. India, the world's second largest-producer of tea, is a nation of one billion tea drinkers, who consume 70% of India's tea output.

India's telecommunication industry is the second-largest in the world with over 1.2 billion subscribers. It contributes 6.5% to India's GDP.[323] After the third quarter of 2017, India surpassed the US to become the second largest smartphone market in the world after China.[324]

The Indian automotive industry, the world's second-fastest growing, increased domestic sales by 26% during 2009–2010,[325] and exports by 36% during 2008–2009.[326] At the end of 2011, the Indian IT industry employed 2.8 million professionals, generated revenues close to US$100 billion equalling 7.5% of Indian GDP, and contributed 26% of India's merchandise exports.[327]

The pharmaceutical industry in India emerged as a global player. As of 2021, with 3000 pharmaceutical companies and 10,500 manufacturing units India is the world's third-largest pharmaceutical producer, largest producer of generic medicines and supply up to 50%—60% of global vaccines demand, these all contribute up to US$24.44 billions in exports and India's local pharmacutical market is estimated up to US$42 billion.[328][329] India is among the top 12 biotech destinations in the world.[330][331] The Indian biotech industry grew by 15.1% in 2012–2013, increasing its revenues from ?204.4 billion (Indian rupees) to ?235.24 billion (US$3.94 billion at June 2013 exchange rates).[332]

Energy

Main articles: Energy in India and Energy policy of India

India's capacity to generate electrical power is 300 gigawatts, of which 42 gigawatts is renewable.[333] The country's usage of coal is a major cause of greenhouse gas emissions by India but its renewable energy is competing strongly.[334] India emits about 7% of global greenhouse gas emissions. This equates to about 2.5 tons of carbon dioxide per person per year, which is half the world average.[335][336] Increasing access to electricity and clean cooking with liquefied petroleum gas have been priorities for energy in India.[337]

Socio-economic challenges

Health workers about to begin another day of immunisation against infectious diseases in 2006. Eight years later, and three years after India's last case of polio, the World Health Organization declared India to be polio-free.[338]

Despite economic growth during recent decades, India continues to face socio-economic challenges. In 2006, India contained the largest number of people living below the World Bank's international poverty line of US$1.25 per day.[339] The proportion decreased from 60% in 1981 to 42% in 2005.[340] Under the World Bank's later revised poverty line, it was 21% in 2011.[l][342] 30.7% of India's children under the age of five are underweight.[343] According to a Food and Agriculture Organization report in 2015, 15% of the population is undernourished.[344][345] The Mid-Day Meal Scheme attempts to lower these rates.[346]

A 2018 Walk Free Foundation report estimated that nearly 8 million people in India were living in different forms of modern slavery, such as bonded labour, child labour, human trafficking, and forced begging, among others.[347] According to the 2011 census, there were 10.1 million child labourers in the country, a decline of 2.6 million from 12.6 million in 2001.[348]

Since 1991, economic inequality between India's states has consistently grown: the per-capita net state domestic product of the richest states in 2007 was 3.2 times that of the poorest.[349] Corruption in India is perceived to have decreased. According to the Corruption Perceptions Index, India ranked 78th out of 180 countries in 2018 with a score of 41 out of 100, an improvement from 85th in 2014.[350][351]

Demographics, languages, and religion

Main articles: Demographics of India, Languages of India, and Religion in India

See also: South Asian ethnic groups

India by language

The language families of South Asia

With 1,210,193,422 residents reported in the 2011 provisional census report,[352] India is the world's second-most populous country. Its population grew by 17.64% from 2001 to 2011,[353] compared to 21.54% growth in the previous decade (1991–2001).[353] The human sex ratio, according to the 2011 census, is 940 females per 1,000 males.[352] The median age was 28.7 as of 2020.[286] The first post-colonial census, conducted in 1951, counted 361 million people.[354] Medical advances made in the last 50 years as well as increased agricultural productivity brought about by the "Green Revolution" have caused India's population to grow rapidly.[355]

The average life expectancy in India is at 70 years—71.5 years for women, 68.7 years for men.[286] There are around 93 physicians per 100,000 people.[356] Migration from rural to urban areas has been an important dynamic in India's recent history. The number of people living in urban areas grew by 31.2% between 1991 and 2001.[357] Yet, in 2001, over 70% still lived in rural areas.[358][359] The level of urbanisation increased further from 27.81% in the 2001 Census to 31.16% in the 2011 Census. The slowing down of the overall population growth rate was due to the sharp decline in the growth rate in rural areas since 1991.[360] According to the 2011 census, there are 53 million-plus urban agglomerations in India; among them Mumbai, Delhi, Kolkata, Chennai, Bangalore, Hyderabad and Ahmedabad, in decreasing order by population.[361] The literacy rate in 2011 was 74.04%: 65.46% among females and 82.14% among males.[362] The rural-urban literacy gap, which was 21.2 percentage points in 2001, dropped to 16.1 percentage points in 2011. The improvement in the rural literacy rate is twice that of urban areas.[360] Kerala is the most literate state with 93.91% literacy; while Bihar the least with 63.82%.[362]

The interior of San Thome Basilica, Chennai, Tamil Nadu. Christianity is believed to have been introduced to India by the late 2nd century by Syriac-speaking Christians.

India is home to two major language families: Indo-Aryan (spoken by about 74% of the population) and Dravidian (spoken by 24% of the population). Other languages spoken in India come from the Austroasiatic and Sino-Tibetan language families. India has no national language.[363] Hindi, with the largest number of speakers, is the official language of the government.[364][365] English is used extensively in business and administration and has the status of a "subsidiary official language";[6] it is important in education, especially as a medium of higher education. Each state and union territory has one or more official languages, and the constitution recognises in particular 22 "scheduled languages".

The 2011 census reported the religion in India with the largest number of followers was Hinduism (79.80% of the population), followed by Islam (14.23%); the remaining were Christianity (2.30%), Sikhism (1.72%), Buddhism (0.70%), Jainism (0.36%) and others[m] (0.9%).[15] India has the third-largest Muslim population—the largest for a non-Muslim majority country.[366][367]

www.ingramcontent.com/pod-product-compliance
Lightning Source LLC
Chambersburg PA
CBHW031425160726
47993CB00003B/1402